'Within this breathless,
clever story, Alex Carul
actions of others exposed to our art. A barely inter-
rupted flow of witty, unreliable interior narrative and
argument left me groping for a handrail; rootless, dis-
turbed and confused as the protagonist.'

Sarah Passingham, author of *Push: My Father, Polio, and Me*

'Fearless storytelling. Dark digressive humour written
with great skill and heaps of energy'

Ashley Hickson-Lovence, author of *The 392*

The Day I Killed J. D. Salinger

Alex Carulli

**Story
Machine**

The Day I Killed J. D. Salinger
Copyright © Alex Carulli 2021

Print ISBN: 9781912665082
Ebook ISBN: 9781912665099
Published by Story Machine, 130 Silver Road,
Norwich, NR3 4TG; www.storymachines.co.uk

Set in Garamond; used under licence.

Printed and bound in the UK by Seacourt Ltd

Story Machine is committed to the environment.
This book is printed using processes that are:

100% carbon positive   100% EMAS   100% renewable energy   100% ISO14001   100% eco-friendly simitri® toner   100% recycled FSC® stock   Zer0% waste to landfill

Printed by **seacourt** – proud to be counted amongst the top environmental printers in the world

The Day I Killed

J. D. Salinger

To the outcasts and outsiders out there

… that rather terrible thing which is there in every photograph: the return of the dead

Roland Barthes

Two days define me: the day I killed J. D. Salinger
and the day of my birth. I was born on December 8
1980 a day that bears great significance and not only
for me or my being or my family or my life but for an
entire generation and for History with a capital H. I
was born in New York City I was born in my
parents' apartment and not in a hospital I was born
alone like few children are nowadays for my mom
was alone at home that night for my father was
working overtime in his deli in downtown Manhattan
for mortgage and debts were rabid dogs hot on their
heels and when I say their I mean my parents' heels
of course not the dogs' also because that wouldn't
make sense would it that imaginary dogs metaphori-
cal dogs were following themselves like a dog chasing
its tail or something and so when my mom alone in
their shabby apartment not too far from the Dakota

Apartments as her personal legend goes heard the five shots shot by MDC—*Why don't you say his name you cowardly little wimp?!*—when she heard the shots at around 11 p.m. on December 8 1980 she began having contractions and went into labor alone in our shabby apartment above a loud bodega whose owner owned the whole block and whose attitude towards immigrants like my parents although an immigrant himself was quite disparaging to say the least making my mom conceal the bump afraid he might kick them out if he'd found out a child was on the way and so imagine how intimidating he was how tough my mom's pregnancy was how impossible it was for her to drag herself downstairs to ask for help that night as MDC pulled the trigger that triggered my mom's labor and pulled me out of her womb into this world a world in which Homo sapiens individuals struggle to be humane humans and the blame-chain of children replicating their parents' shortcomings their violence their dysfunction is never-ending and— *Stop this nonsense: this is our chance to escape! Now that they're changing all doors and windows! Come on Ros! They're at the top floor now and'll be here soon maybe in an hour or two. Get ready get ready get ready I say!* Soon after the contractions began my mom phoned my father at the deli though the phone kept ringing ringing ringing in the empty dark shop ringing echoing reverberating unpicked and these solitary sound waves mingled with the buzzzzzzzzz of refrigerators and freezers and brushed the Italian goods on the shelves but didn't reach couldn't possibly reach my father's ears as he walked home as he usually did also to work out a little or else I'll look pregnant myself as he kept saying even after I was born and until he got semi-retired and had to shelve that habit too along with overtime and smoking and so since my mom at the time did not speak English she slammed the receiver down on the cradle though she did not know it was called cradle and I doubt she knows it even today for the only cradle she knew if she did know was her fetus's and she did not call the hospital or the midwifery clinic or even the few fellow Italian women she knew back then and thank god she wasn't religious which is why she didn't think of calling those overly stuffy pious old-fashioned women on the catholic holy day of the Immaculate Conception no less and thought it best to sit on her immaculate towel-covered bed with cellophane-wrapped mattress crying her eyes out suffering in deep indescribable pain alone suffering alone and in a break between contractions she turned the radio on so that it could cover her screaming and shouting in the middle of the night and avoid the landlord downstairs hearing her and getting suspicious getting upstairs uninvited getting involved and right then right from the radio's creaky halting loudspeakers came the unsettling announcement of John Lennon's assassination and a few minutes later I was born. *Always with this boring story! Boring! Boring!*

Fucking boring! Shut up shut up shut up! So technically I was born on December 9 but my mother who heard the radio's breaking news but didn't understand a word of it came to know about the murder by my father who told her John Lennon had died in the very Roosevelt Hospital they had taken me after my birth shot at the Dakota Apartments not too far from their shabby apartment so right then my mother who loved the Beatles taken aback and sad and shocked told my father to tell the hospital people I was born just when the shots were fired which was at about 11 p.m. on December 8 (—*KNOCK KNOCK!* —)

Yes?

May I come in?

I recognize the voice through the door the voice of suave handsome velvety-skinned Dr. McVain.

Of course I say come on in. I like talking to him and I think he has a teenage crush on me only we are no teenagers we are both adults but him being the patient doctor and me being the impertinent patient it means we can flirt a little which we do now and again. He's not exactly new here he's been here a few months now but I feel a special connection with him that has made me open up.

How are you feeling today Rossana?

Sometimes he calls me by my full former name and I love hearing it come out of his mouth. *You bitch! Tell him tell him!*

I was wondering if you wished to continue the conversation we left unfinished yesterday. It was so interesting and illuminating.

Tell him! Tell him! I'm sorry Doctor McVain. Yes sure of course I'd love to carry on talking. Just remind me where we left off.

Well you'd mentioned the movie Trainspotting as an example of what you were saying because you said many young friends of yours tried and were subsequently hooked on heroin after watching the 1996 movie and that many died too.

Oh yes I say and like a fast-flowing river the rapids a waterfall the words and ideas we exchanged the day before flood my mind. That movie I say exalted heroin and made many of my friends die very young.

Well Dr. McVain says since you mentioned some movies as examples of works of art that created violence and escaped responsibility though in your opinion they shouldn't be allowed to do so I did a little research and read an interesting interview with Stanley Kubrick whom you mentioned as well.

Right I say.

If I'm not wrong Dr. McVain says you said you admire Kubrick as a movie director also because of I seem to remember his photographic eye.

You have such a great memory doc I say with a languid smile I wipe off my face immediately afraid it might betray mine was also a slight innuendo.

I write things down he shows me his notebook with his lovely humble smile. I'd like to read you a passage from an interview to Kubrick in response to the accusations he'd received about A Clockwork Orange encouraging violence and delinquency. And now the doctor reads from his notebook on his lap: To attribute powerful suggestive qualities to a film is at odds with the scientifically accepted view that even after deep hypnosis in a post-hypnotic state people cannot be made to do things which are at odds with their natures. That's what Kubrick said.

The doc stops and stares at me as he often does and I like the way he looks at me because it makes me feel interesting like I truly have something worthwhile to say though I have to say I never failed to notice a faint hint of condescension in his look but that's not particularly surprising coming from a man and a doctor and we women know this kind of attitude only too well don't we?

Maybe because I don't say anything Dr. McVain clears his throat and says What Kubrick said is exactly what I mean when I say you can't hold a movie or a work of art responsible for the actions of individuals. Art reproduces life the doc says art unravels life but it does not create it.

It does I say and I think it's undeniable actually.

Okay he says. Since you keep saying that and you have a soft spot for John Lennon and the Beatles then please tell me what about Helter Skelter and the

Manson Family's murders?

What about them?

Shouldn't the Beatles have withdrawn the White Album from commerce because of the hidden messages Charles Manson claimed to have deciphered in it?

Whether we like it or not art always conveys messages. And what the point of reception grasps is not always what the source of emission means. However once it's out there a work of art speaks and the artist is responsible for what it says. So maybe the Beatles should have stopped playing those particular songs and invested them with a different meaning.

Do you really believe it was the songs' hidden messages that told Manson to incite those kids to go on a murdering spree?

I think Charles Manson was seeking and finding confirmation of his own racist theory in the Beatles' songs rather than being inspired by them.

Do you realize how much more lenient you are with the Beatles than with J. D. Salinger?

Oh come on Doctor McVain. A year after the murders the Beatles disbanded.

Surely not because of—

J. D. fucking Salinger was a phony! He did nothing to take responsibility! Nothing zilch nix nada! He just hid and was too chickenshit to even face a harmless biographer who—
And to get back to Stanley Kubrick: after having refused several times to withdraw his movie

following the explosion of copycat gang violence he gave in doc he did and A Clockwork Orange wasn't shown in any movie theater for decades.

But Ros that doesn't mean he accepted that there is a connection between violence in movies or art and violence in society. Kubrick and his wife had received death threats. So he was scared and wanted to protect his wife and himself. I know you had a similarly serious and challenging experience with one of your shots.

Which I destroyed without hesitation or regrets right after I came to know the tragedy it had caused.

I know and I feel for you I really do. But…

Did you know I say that some Camorra boss in Napoli or something had his mansion his palace built like an exact replica of the residence of Tony Montana from the movie Scarface?

That's delusion of grandeur Ros plain and simple. I cure patients with that disturb.

All right all right I say so let's forget for a minute about the violent and negative effects and let's focus on art in general on its intrinsic strength its positive and liberating effects on societies. Art establishes new canons of beauty and demolishes old ones. Art helps humans in their quest for spiritual elevation or introspective evaluation. It's simply undeniable that art has a paramount function in societies which makes it a political and moral agent and as such responsible for its impact. *Oh look at those lips! Bite them! Bite them! Aarrgh!*

Marta he says. Can I talk to you?

Are you trying to change the subject? I say.

It's not art per se that changes people he says. It's the ideas and ideals within it that urge people to do things.

That's exactly what I'm saying doctor. So we finally agree: art does create life. Art shapes life.

No Ros. What I mean is that whatever you do be that a good or a bad deed it's your conscience and the beliefs and morals you have interiorized that make you take a path instead of another. Not a work of art.

But these beliefs don't come out of nowhere doc. Culture informs our mores and outlook on life.

Listen Ros in The Catcher in the Rye J. D. Salinger spoke of a generational malaise maybe a widespread angst among the youngsters of the time maybe about his own experience as a youth et cetera but he did not tell Mark David Chapman to go kill John Lennon. And anyway you cannot hold the writer responsible for what a deranged man who by his own admission wanted to become famous one way or the other has done after reading his book. Which by the way was read by many other millions of people in the world and no one went killing anyone except for Mark David Chapman.

That's not entirely true— *You hear you hear? He says his name he does but why can't you eh? Why not? You wimp! You pussy!*

Marta is it okay for me to talk to you for a minute?
Dr. McVain says.

Yes! No doctor I say she's gone and she's not
coming back. *The hell I'm not! You loser loser!* I know
doctor you may not understand me or sympathize
with me because after all I am a murderer just like
MDC—*You see? You can't say his fucking name you
moronic fool!*—Shut up shut up! But doc what that man
did and the consequences of his actions are all
embedded in me like morals and so I am what I am
and who I am also because I was born the day I was
born and I'm not talking about synchronicity here
I'm talking about the fact my mom was never the
same after that and even if she managed to re-emerge
from the abysmal depths of baby blues and
postpartum and depression and whatever unhappy
sea or ocean or torrent or swamp she found herself
in after my birth she carried that tragedy in her blood
and in her bones and therefore I carried it in mine.
*What a shitload of crappy whimpers and whines! Let's get out
of here already!* Enough now I say and roll my eyes and
without knowing where it comes from I follow an
urge to jump on Dr. McVain and kiss him and tell
him I love him though it's not true even if I do have
feelings for him and I'd certainly like to ride him and
so I put my hands on his muscular thighs and
squeeze them and I want to dive mouth on dick and
blow him suck him suck him slurpy breathless slutty
lusty and swallow him all but he rears up springs up

looks down at and *on* me who then retreat in shame with downcast eyes with the desire the only desire to evaporate disappear vanish. He asks me if I'm all right but I don't answer I just stay silent giving him my back as I have done a few times before so he knows what I mean and he also knows he has to leave but before doing that as he often does he reassures me that I don't have to worry or feel bad or ashamed about it because these violent outbursts of impetuous sexual drive these mad impulses these primal instincts taking over my rational being my ego controlling my id which in the end is made of base basic instincts like the Sharon Stone movie isn't it he says not to worry for these feral sexual eruptions are typical side effects of the meds I take which come to think of it are the only things except food and water I am allowed to swallow in here.

Sometimes I hate Marta's rude manic interruptions. And what's with this escape thing? Where do we go? and why? I'm not saying I'm fine here and all that but once we leave here if we do leave here which I don't think it's going to happen though I'm more than happy to consider it once we leave here where do we go where in this cruel world this unjust world this racist classist patriarchal world where do we go where would we be accepted for who we are with no questions asked no doubts or eyebrows raised and no need to fix us no need to decipher through the ignominious nomenclature of science whose science? our entangled personalities where would we go where is this place where no one would try to associate libellous labels with our disassociation and no one would try to formalize categorize DSM-ize and finally institutionalize our wild wilderness where the hell is this place if there is such a place different from hell which I doubt. And escaping this place this institution this nuthouse this loony bin as they were called some time ago after ten years would make us no good and would only increase our sense of marginalisation in whatever peripheries or suburbs of the mind also the collective mind the culture our broken fragmentary lives end up unfolding.

When I was little I remember my parents used to talk about their migrating to the States from Italy and they said it felt wrong at times it felt as if they were betraying something not their country or their people nothing like that because my parents were not patriotic actually quite the contrary but they said it felt as though they were betraying other people's expectations betraying the sibyls and clairvoyants betraying the alleged natural course of events betraying the resigned fatalism they thought was so ingrained in and characteristic of poor bumpkinish working-class people especially Italians especially Southerners especially peasants like themselves. They often said they felt mutilated by their departure and

they felt they could never belong to either country
though they cared to point out they didn't
particularly care but that I Rossana as they called me
I needed to know where I came from what feelings
and emotions and turmoil my parents had harbored
because of their decision and of the tough ambivalent
existential condition that inevitably befalls migrants
immigrants refugees foreigners strangers outsiders
outcasts misfits the solitude the displacement of self
the all-devouring fear of being antagonized ostracized
marginalized the magnitude of otherness the guilt.
And when my parents arrived in the States it was the
late Seventies when the Cold War ever sly sneaky
sleazy and ever-present even after the Vietnam War
which still reverberated in the air in the leaden
atmosphere made joyful colorful and lively only by
the hippies and their revolutionary movement their
moving revolution which unfortunately failed
miserably the Cold War didn't allow nuances gray
areas middle ways and demanded of people they be
either with or against something an entity a
philosophy a social-economic system which no one
really grasped deep down to its minutiae but
everyone liked to exploit so my mother told me the
assassination of John Lennon was a shock a spiritual
tremor a lingering threat that she had been terrified
by for weeks and weeks on end and not because she
feared for her life or my dad's or mine but because
she felt that was some kind of watershed and that the

explosion of the Third World War a nuclear war between the USA and the USSR would have been less shocking for the assassination of John Lennon was a historical event that pierced the soul the spirit my mother's intimacy and that of millions more and therefore it was not a political act but a direct attack against individuality not individualism against a sense of shared intimacy the knowing feeling that others experience the same inner unbalanced turbulence which songs like those of John Lennon were able to soothe and put into context and it felt like my mother told me it felt like that terrible incident was there to remind everyone no one was safe not even in their own passions in their own houses at the Dakota Apartments like John and Yoko or the shabby apartment of my parents Gianni and Marina because fame and the desire to be famous at all costs the thirst for fame the greed which follow the fame famine that also MDC had experienced and wanted to assuage were bound to compose the future world's intercultural anthem its credo its motto.

At my birthday parties when after the cake we watched the slides of the previous year's party with the slide projector beaming its light against the bare wall in the dark living room I would unfailingly be saddened by my mom's gloomy grim nostalgic heavy facial expression both in the pictures of the year before when she and I and everyone else in the whole world were a year younger and in the flesh on

the face of the person sitting next to me and I knew she was sad because my birthday reminded her of John Lennon's death. I guess what I'm trying to say here is that I sort of grew up with a kind of indirect obsession which grew bigger and bigger when—
Fucking boriiiiiiiing! Jesus Christ Ros! No wonder no one wants to fuck you. You're such a pussy such a bore such an inconsequential chatterbox with a one-track mind and you like to talk talk talk and you end up with turning people off. You yackety-yak yak yak endlessly and with no end. Jeez. I know how it went and why we did what we did and there's no need to excuse or justify yourself because you and I are like art like the black-and-white pictures you've become famous for and just like your photographs we don't need to mean something we and our actions don't need to carry any specific meaning we just are like art just is. So let me recount how and what went down on January 27 2010 ten years ago the day we ended up here which is as I would have called it The day WE killed J. D. Salinger. And Ros I know you say as you said to Dr. McVain a couple of times though afterwards you didn't seem to remember I showed up only a few days before our most splendid feat our utmost contribution to this humanity although to be honest I don't give a shit don't give a fuck about humanity but it makes me feel proud to have contributed with such a ground-breaking time-defining time-defying act an act which we incubated for months no matter what you say about me showing up only some days before and carried out meticulously. And Ros don't listen to that charming handsome superfuckable doctor when he says this is all the product of our

fucked-up imagination our hallucinations our delusions and that it is quite peculiar I remember him saying it is quote quite peculiar that both you and Marta lie about this event unquote as if it is actually weird that a crucial pivotal central essential event in someone's life an event that has helped multiply the blurry personalities a complex woman hoards within should stay intact and pure and not be affected by itself. He is a man and men tend to diminish us especially when they are threatened by our strength our character our determination our balls as they call it which reveals their limitedness their machismo their condescension. Now let me explain. *Fuck explaining!* Up until college I felt for my depressed mother but did nothing to alleviate her to alleviate her suffering I just brooded over her state and accepted her condition as immutable and inescapable and derived from her sacrifice-prone essence the Old Country's genetic inheritance the Southern Italian peasants' near-religious acquiescence in the face of adversity and injustice which I thought I would inherit and find within myself sooner or later and so I accepted her dark presence until I began seeing it as the prison the cage the shape of life I had the moral obligation to deform and escape from. *Let's escape from here goddamn it! Let's do it now!* Like breaking the blame-chain breaking the circle the unvirtuous vicious circle the counter-revolutionary revolving doors of the previous generation's oversights misjudgements mistakes missed chances.

I reasoned that the first thing I had to do if I

wanted to help my mom face her ghosts was to understand who she really was and to do that I had to visit her birthplace. So right after my film video and photographic arts major at NYU I moved to Southern Italy where I lived for nearly one and a half years in my parents' village living cheap healthy and slooooow like you have no idea. There I honed my photographic skills and built a strong conceptual symbolic edifice around them. Unlike other art forms like writing or painting photography and also film-making though the latter is a natural consequence of the technical development of the former photography needs the external world to be there and be the object of its art: there is no photography without a person an animal a flower a river a landscape a building a road a cloud there is no photography of our feelings and the only way to express them through photography is to have something or someone outside ourselves that can incarnate them. Nevertheless it is the art form most faithful to reality to the real world and real feelings for no writer or painter not even the great masters of the past can convey on page or on canvas or in marble or on stage the emotional intensity and profundity of say a photograph of a real-life mother crying as she holds her real-life dead child. An art form capable of freezing a juncture in time and space capable of capturing an unrepeatable moment snatched off the otherwise unbreakable fluid

continuum be it circular or linear we call existence
and capable of reproducing that moment ad
infinitum. So what I did was I challenged this
unchallengeable concept by trying to capture the
overabundant emptiness the stillness the ancient
repose of the unpeopled landscape not inhospitable
nor hostile which I learned that swiftly and
seamlessly becomes the landscape of the mind of the
soul. And when I once took a shot of a cloudless
blue sky with only a hawk in the distance barely
visible in the top right corner more than a raptor a
blemish against that oppressively solid sky and
showed the black-and-white print to some people in
my parents' home town I knew I was on the right
track because their puzzled expressions betrayed a
sense of shameful familiarity as though their
bafflement was nothing but a defence mechanism a
shielding veneer a mask worn in reaction to the
subtle exposure of their dull empty lonely immutable
existence. I went on shooting mainly natural patterns
with geometric or completely abstract shapes and
lines and then during the last two or three months
concentrated solely on portraits: of farmers cops
youngsters oldsters toothless barflies but especially of
old women with faces like road maps furrowed like
ready-to-get-sowed fields local old women whom I
had seen trotting around the village ever-busy with
their bandy legs and slight hunchbacks like humanoid
spinning tops who reminded me what my mom

would look like in thirty forty years had she stayed there. I realized that if I hadn't dedicated almost an entire year to photographing nothingness looking for meaning in voids of significance in chasms of plainness in abysses of inscrutable stasis I would have never been able to capture the depth of the portraits I put together under the title Landscapes of the Mind which two years later became my breakthrough project the shots that set off my artistic career the shots every gallery in Europe was eager to make theirs the shots that eventually allowed me to drop out of NYU where I had returned in vain as it turned out for an MA. I had moved to my parents' birthplace to see the Old Country to see where my parents came from to meet my grandparents my uncles and aunties my cousins their husbands their wives and their children and my great-uncles and great-aunts the primary school my parents attended the church they went to and were tacitly excommunicated by and all the places that served as settings for all the stories I'd heard in my childhood like the watering troughs in which they dived and swam as children the pinewood with the tree houses they played in the wheat fields where they hid and ran and fooled around with flea-bitten stray dogs the slaughterhouse with its noisome stench the deconsecrated church with its spooky graveyard the soccer field where my dad never played a game but took part in many a tale of derring-do… but I had

also moved there to try to root out the canker of my
supposed roots which without my uprooted parents
seemed utterly sapless lifeless merely vestigial an
empty concept a misbelief a rural myth and to try to
root out the big little traumas the incomprehensions
the incompatibilities the frictions between my parents
and that genuine simple touchy unpretentious remote
dullsville humorless universe with backwards ways
which is the emotional baggage my parents stoically
hauled around even though it had scarred them and
pushed them away. And if I had succeeded in
enhancing my photographic abilities I most definitely
failed in grasping a sense of belonging of intangible
attachment to that place and its people a sense of
inherited communion with that way of life and their
morals and ethics and customs. Near the end and
before I embarked on the Landscapes of the Mind
project I desperately longed to go back to New York
I missed it so much I missed its colors its noise its
life its vibrancy and speed and hustle and was so fed
up with being stared at so blatantly so rudely so
unabashedly by everyone both animals and humans
of all sexes and ages. *Jesus fucking Christ kill me now!*
Are you ever gonna stop?! I told you there's only one thing we
should do now and that's escape from this fucking place! So—
When I got back home to New York my growing
renown kind of preceded me. Not that people
recognized me on the street or stopped me to take a
selfie or stuff like that also because back then there

were no selfies and cell phones didn't take pictures
and back then if the photographer wanted to be
included in the shot she had to use the self-timer
which delayed the opening of the shutter so no
nothing like a celebrity also because I truly honestly
viscerally loathe artists who act like celebs even those
like J. D. Salinger who are or were I should say
famous for the very fact they didn't want to be
famous. By then I had gotten rid of the sane part of
my name and went simply by Ros or R.O.S. as I sign
my works and that was the name that began popping
up on the cover of this and that art magazine and so
the few people who still called me Rossana were my
parents and old family friends and the incurably
pedantic bureaucrats we have foolishly entrusted with
the power of ruling over us.

Ros? It's Doctor McVain again. Sorry to bother
you. May I come in?

Yes please do.

He comes in and I think maybe he changed his
mind and having thrown his deontological ethics down
the toilet he wants to jump on me and fuck me good
and hard but no damn it I am mistaken because he is
not a fucking fickle fucker so I have to resort once
again to digital penetration which is no analog of anal
intercourse of course though I think I'm veering off
course so I'd better get back to it and listen to what his
sexy lips ever so rosy ever so silky like his voice are
saying which is When I saw you before I forgot to tell

you that as you must know we are changing all doors and windows. You'll be happy to know the building will be thoroughly insulated so no more drafty rooms plus we've managed to fit all windows with much-needed two-way mirrors so you residents will always be able to see outside but no one will be able to see inside.

Holy fuck doc! Shut up I say. So when are they going to change my window?

Either this afternoon or tomorrow morning. I'm not sure yet.

And where do I go what do I do while they work in here?

Well there's plenty to do as you well know.

Yeah we can go to the communal recreational room… whatchamacallit…? The game room that purgatorio that antechamber the terribly smelly vestibule of the slaughterhouse.

Can I talk to you Marta?

Go ahead doc. You don't know it yet but you've met your match.

Right. So what is it that you think of the things that Ros and I have discussed?

Wow doc I can tell you were fast asleep when they taught writing composition in school. I can't believe Marta has actually made Dr. McVain laugh out loud.

You're right he says that was quite a poorly stated sentence. So let me rephrase it: what do you think of Ros's idea of art having a huge influence on life?

Form is better but as per content my dear doc I'm afraid you still need to improve. Anyway I absolutely agree with her and that's why we did what we did. Killing that phony J. D. Salinger just like his character liked to call everybody else but his own creator is the best thing Ros and I have ever done. I know that action sent us here but—

Sorry to interrupt you. What would you say if I told you that J. D. Salinger died of natural causes in Cornish New Hampshire roughly five hours away from your loft in Brooklyn?

I'd say we know how long it takes to get there because we drove that distance that very day. Only because you don't believe us it doesn't mean we didn't do what we have been found guilty of.

Okay. So what if I told you no judge ever sentenced you for murder and that there are documents I can show you that prove you were in Brooklyn that night before you… you were hospitalized and then sent here?

I'd say you're full of shit. I'd say show us the docs doc and we'll see. I'd say you should be ashamed of yourself for trying to take advantage of us and our weakness fondling us groping us touching our tits and asses sticking your finger up our assholes and pussies and making us suck your dick with the threat of—

W-what the hell is this? Stop this nonsense now. What are you trying to do?

I'm just saying you gotta stop molesting us. We are your patients and we confide in you we trust you and you exploit our trust you betray our trust your sneaky predator!

Sorry Doctor McVain I don't know what— *Wait*

until the hashtag StopPredatorDrMcVain gets top trending and you'll see.

You will do nothing of the kind!

We have no phone or computer I say so don't worry Doctor McVain she's just fooling around she's just trying to scare you for fun. She does not mean any of this she is not serious and you know it.

Dr. McVain pale trembling shaken leaves my room and for some reason I pull the gym bag out of the closet and quickly hastily in a frenzy fill it with some clothes my notebooks and the framed photograph of my parents and dash out of the room with Marta whispering to me what I have to do where I have to go which corridor I have to take which to avoid and… *avoid the elevator and take the stairs and act natural don't show we're running but keep on striding with confidence so that no one doubts our sense of purpose our determination and before reaching the basement where we will steal a car perhaps even Dr. McVain's car so we make the theft a symbolic one let's sneak into a doctor's office and steal one of their white coats so that from the distance no nurse no security moron will notice we are who we are and not a doctor on her way to the basement where she'll get into her car and— VROOM!—out of here once and for all.* As we walk with a steady pace cautious and soft feline and stealthy and Marta's voice floats suasive in my head we recall what Dr. McVain once told us that not only did we have a selective memory pretty much like everybody else but that we also had quite an exquisitely selective amnesia. He said it's peculiar that all we remember is somehow connected to John Lennon MDC and J. D. Salinger and his infamous book and its protagonist Holden Caulfield and his hate for phonies which is the very hatred MDC shared with him and it's strange Dr. McVain said it's rather strange that the two points limiting the segment that is our life before coming to this place are murders. We never found this particularly strange or odd or peculiar to be honest for the simple fact we *are* murderers so what the hell does he think we are going to be defined by if not murders? So down to the basement we go after we've paid a visit to a doctor's office antiseptic empty claustrophobic and have stolen a white coat and put it on and grinned with self-satisfaction at our reflection in the mirror or rorrim as I used to call it back in college and we hazard the sad conclusion an induction more than a deduction that you can in fact judge a book by its cover because we do look like a doctor don't we in this white coat with our ponytailed hair with bangs all neat and clean and glossy like we could write our own ticket because respectability comes with presentability which comes at a price whose affordability comes with the availability of resources at one's disposal which often are the prerogative of the long-established well-respected rich who restrict access to their exclusive clubs and resources and decide what is and what is not respectable morally acceptable tolerable frowned

upon conceded condoned condemned and translate
these principles into canons and customs and rituals
and laws terrible unjust unfair unlawful laws which
enter and penetrate permeate life and existence and
slowly become so entrenched that people forget that
those dictates and tenets are in fact arbitrary choices
made by the self-styled God's anointed the self-
appointed authorities the self-centered centralists the
vainglorious crème de la crème gone sour rancid
rotten yet still on top of the cake like icing with no
intention to melt down and yield their privilege for
no one's sake but their small elite's.

   We are about to break into a car maybe Dr.
McVain's maybe not who really cares when we
realize we do not know how to start it and how to
hot-wire it as they say and if it's even possible to do
so with these new cars with electronic key fobs and
all their gimmicky contactless apparatus. But right
then we see an old station wagon entering the
underground parking lot reserved to doctors
personnel and visitors and once the old man has
parked his car we approach him and tell him we have
lost our car key but we need a car for an emergency
and when he says What about calling an ambulance?
we are quick on the trigger and it's actually Marta
who's quick on the trigger and she goes *It's a personal
emergency not a professional one. Are you here to visit a
relative or a friend?* she asks with calm politeness which
doesn't really suit her if you ask me but does the job

all the same and the old man says Yes I'm Joyce Finnegan's father.

Joyce! Marta says. *What a good and well-meaning woman she is. Well if you could be so kind to lend me your car for half an hour or so it would be much appreciated. I'll work the night shift today so…*

The old man is hesitant doubt visibly squeezing his wrinkly forehead he does not know what to do torn between selfish mistrust of the human race and selfless generosity and deference demanded by the alleged emergency situation and the white coat's status symbol and the respectability and compliance it invokes.

Gotta go back home in a coupla hours tops so make sure you're here on time doc the old man says.

Couple of hours? You kidding? I'm on duty here. This is my shift. I'll be back in no time. Thank you sir thank you very much you're so kind and understanding. No wonder you're Joyce's dad.

We drive off and see the loony bin grow smaller in the rearview mirror and then past the gates we turn right onto a tree-lined road and we start thinking about that gullible old man father of bad loser Joyce tearful Joyce moody shabby booger-eating Joyce and somehow my father's face pops up and the way he might have been hustled into things he did not want to do like this old man here giving us his old jalopy. But you know my father's life as an immigrant who by no means liked to play the victim quite the opposite to be honest my parents' life's hardship is not a woeful account of deprivation misery poverty scruffy clothes and shabby apartments like the one they lived in and in which I was born on December 8 1980 as you all well know by now. Their second-class citizens' life their untranslatable struggle is replete with the ever-present timid fear of dissenting and speaking-up the strict avoidance of dissenting protesting contesting not to appear ungrateful or unappreciative towards the welcoming country which welcomed them to exploit them let's face it though the country itself was and is subjugated to a system the capitalistic system and therefore one can consider the country's laziness passivity and negligence as products of its inherent naïvety. Replete with the perceived illegitimacy of their mute complaints and the unspeakable unspoken impracticable proscription of new customs unavoidable customs like eating standing and forget about hour-long sit-down lunches sacred and oily interspersed with food talk forget about courses served in rigid logical order nutritionally sound order if a little self-righteously rigid and eat everything in one big plate hot and cold mixed up sweet and sour mixed up cooked and raw. Forget about blood red vino and welcome fizzy cola and other sugary pops sporting fruit names on their labels alack unaware of the true taste color and flavor of the fruits whose names and more or less stylized images they bear. And so my parents being unreligious and all were outsiders among the

outsiders they were the unbelievers among the
believers they were the unprincipled among the self-
proclaimed principled Italians who hung out
principally with Italians in Italian neighborhoods and
went to Italian churches at Italian holidays and to
Italian restaurants Italian shops Italian delis like my
father's though they dared not stay longer than
necessary and never engaged in small talk with him
who didn't really care so the Italians guided by
superstitious clichés and prejudice discriminated the
disgraziati of my parents not only for being too weird
and unorthodox and deviant for a couple of
Southern peasants with their only daughter me the
sweet *burratina* as they called me unbaptized impure
unfreed from the original sin and thus bound to go
to inferno not only for this but also for hanging out
with people from the African American community
the blacks though the Wops and Dagos used a much
more offensive term which I'm not going to repeat
and so it went that my parents kept to themselves my
parents didn't have a real social life didn't integrate
nor did they disintegrate much to many racist bettors'
disappointment. And I have to thank the deep sense
of alienation thrust upon them if I have become what
I have become. I have to thank my ignorant mother
if I've become the renowned photographer I am: I
still remember the day in my senior year when what I
wanted to be when I grew up became absolutely
blindingly clear to me like the sun peeping out of a

thick mass of gray clouds and washing the whole world anew with light. I had spent the Christmas holidays taking photographs around the hood and used all the money I had saved from my allowance to print and frame two of the pictures. I remember getting back home one afternoon after school and after having gone to the print-and-frame shop to collect my two first ever serious works of art and I remember being overwhelmed with agitation trepidation exaltation expectation elation perturbation unabating palpitations and then I showed the works to my mom and as soon as she expressed her comment I knew I would become a photographer no matter what. I recall her sad unsmiling face light up her facial muscles relax her eyes brighten up and then she said in Italian though I'll say it in English she said Oh finally! Well done Rossana. Finally something that speaks American but that I can understand! I loved her so much for that so much because she made me realize once and for all that my duty as an artist also on her behalf was to speak up for people like her like my father like me the outcasts the outsiders the underprivileged the alienated the dispossessed the marginalized speak up for them through an art form that transcends language and that— *When the fuck are you gonna thank me for what we've done what we've accomplished?! You thank this and that but not a single word of praise for me. I am the one who helped us achieve our greatest goal. I am the one who stole that second-hand book from that bookshop and read it all in one sitting. Ian Hamilton's In Search of J. D. Salinger the book that helped us make the decision to fucking act instead of moaning and complaining about how irresponsible and cowardly that J. D. Salinger was for not having taken his life for what he had done with his fucking book and his attitude of reclusive show-off. Go on Ros. Praise me for once. Praise me for luring Joyce's dad into giving us his car. Go on. And tell the whole story about January 27. If you don't I will. But if I do I do not want you to interrupt me or complain or start correcting me or shit like that. Okay? Once I start there ain't no stopping me. You know that.*

So here's what happened that fateful day the day WE killed J. D. Salinger.

We had already entertained the idea of killing him and weeks had gone by with us brooding over the matter and its implications. We were mainly concerned with practical implications rather than moral or legal ones. The how and when and what with et cetera. So I think it was January 25 and we were browsing second-hand books in a small independent bookstore down in Williamsburg when we found Ian Hamilton's volume and deemed the discovery an omen too coincidental to be merely coincidental. And even though we were not afraid of getting caught because we thought we were doing humanity a solid a fucking service and therefore did not even consider that eventuality we nonetheless acted like criminals should and stole the book so there would be no trace of us buying it. We read it in one sitting that very night. It was the last straw: the next day we planned the action and carried it out the day after that. We reached Cornish New Hampshire and were surprised at the easiness with which we could approach J. D. Salinger's residence. The infamous jeep was there the jeep even Hamilton talked about the jeep seen by many reporters and another car too. Maybe his wife's. Do you really need to say all this? *No interruptions. You promised.* No I didn't. And I don't think we should be dwelling on these past events and going into details and all that. Suffice it to say we got there and entered the place and killed the old phony. *No no no! We have to put it down in words down in black and white actually to use an expression so apt so dear to you the black-and-white fundamentalist we have to say it loud and clear that we looked the old bastard in the eye the man being heartier and less wrinkly than we expected and in direct contradiction with what was said in the press an allusion to a* sudden decline [of his health] after the new year. *He was still standing on his legs when we shot him right between his eyes and saw him collapse at our feet in a pool of blood his corpse finally prostrate and subdued and—* Stop it! Stop it! I am not comfortable with you telling that story… *Oh come on you chicken you wimp you pussy!* But Marta admit it it's all blurry cloudy misty foggy hazy and even painful for taking someone's life is a dreadful business and not an easy burden to carry not an easy stain to erase from your soul not an easy lump to swallow even if the victim deserved it even if you are not a guilt-prone individual. Besides I care about it for what it spurred in me not for what it was like doing it how

complicated or fun or easy it was not for the pedantic
petty practicalities the morbid interest in gory details
not for love for the sensationalistic angle or angel. I
remember it because the day I killed J. D. Salinger I
was reborn.

It may come as a surprise to you me being a
professional photographer derivatively obsessed with
MDC and John Lennon to know that I had not seen
the infamous picture taken by Paul Goresh a few
hours before the assassination and that only when I
kind of chanced upon it on the internet did I realize
what could be done to avenge my mom and her
suffering her pain her depression: wipe MDC's grin
off his face wipe it off that very photograph and off
history's face at least symbolically and give that grin a
new connotation. Now take that picture and look at
it closely look at it carefully examine it. For a second
forget what's happening there that is John Lennon
autographing a copy of his Double Fantasy album for
his killer. Forget that and see how Lennon appears as
though his eyes are peacefully closed his head bent
down in humble obsequiousness a bow given to a
sated grimacing devilish modern-day putto. Roland
Barthes said that a photograph has the ability to
resurrect the dead so when I saw that picture and I
saw John Lennon alive again something in my head
went *click!* and *ding!* and *dong!* and *bang!* and then

finally I heard a voice a woman's soothing voice a voice I had never heard before whispering in my ear whispering softly a desire a wish a sweet graphic instruction that crept into my mind and remolded rearranged my thoughts like a mother's advice does to her children's priorities. And I know that Dr. McVain says these are the exact same things MDC said about himself and what went on in his head that day the day I was born. I know MDC talked about voices in his head and the Little People controlling him guiding his actions and telling him Do it do it do it until he fucking did it but as you must have noticed Marta and I have a completely different relationship for neither of us is subject to the other neither subjugates or leads the other: we are two but we are one and as one we do what we do unanimously. So when we read in Ian Hamilton's book what J. D. Salinger had done to all the reporters biographers and scholars who wanted to know more about him and his work denying even a fair use of his material denying interviews denying explanations publications re-editions and indeed suing some of them we came to the conclusion that we could if not straighten history at least have it rectified and have the wrongdoers make reparation to their victims. By killing J. D. Salinger we aimed to do what he himself should have done in the first place as a judicious response to the wicked deed his book's character had elicited. Also we aimed to give justice to my mom and incidentally the world by sacrificing him at the altar of causality and responsibility. So we reasoned If we kill him we show other irresponsible artists they should bear the consequences of their actions and artistic choices. Besides we would orphan Holden Caulfield and by association by inference also Mark David Fucking Chapman— *Attagirl! You said it! You fucking did it Ros!*

Dr. McVain has quite an annoying irritating take in this regard. He believes there is no overlapping no superposition between the artist and the human between in my case the photographer and the woman between the writer and the man in J. D. Salinger's case. Dr. McVain thinks there is a clear-cut separation between the two entities and that one does not or at least should not be confused with the other. I find it ironic that I do not see the separation and he does though it appears he sees duplicity and disassociation everywhere… as if he saw double all the time… He says that what the artist does should not reflect on the individual and the individual should not be held accountable for what the artist has done. Which is a load of bullshit if you ask me. I suspect he came up with this idea only to contradict me and check out my reaction. So basically he thinks we should not have killed J. D. Salinger the man because it was J. D. Salinger the writer who created Holden Caulfield et cetera. And I recall Dr. McVain saying he would have accepted our murderous endeavor far more easily if theoretically speaking we had targeted the author somehow and not the man who Dr. McVain believes should be left alone once the product of his intellectual work has left him and has become part of a society's culture of human knowledge of humanity's legacy. *Fuck that!* I remember Marta telling him with her usual diplomacy.

I understand everyone wants to avoid taking her work home but there are some kinds of jobs that don't allow you to do that and being an artist is one of them: the artist's responsibility toward society toward the world she is trying to deconstruct and reconstruct on the basis of her own art's statements and intrinsic philosophy or socio-political angle the responsibility of what she does and how she does it and why and when and maybe even where stays with her and is undetachable from her and her life outside the artistic world. Art forms the texture of the edge on which it runs along the edge between real and fake true and false right and wrong light and shadow black and white. So artists have to take sides when they are asked to and the individual inhabiting the artist cannot just shrug off her responsibility claiming that her art and herself are two distinct entities two distinct vehicles of two distinct sentiments.

In summer 2009 to advertise my upcoming solo show at a prestigious gallery the gallery curator and I picked one of my shots and had its enlargement displayed on twenty-five billboards across the city. The black-and-white shot was titled Integration Or How To Lick Your Pals Into Shape and depicted the patka-wearing Indian boy who used to live across the street from my loft in Brooklyn licking an overexposed vanilla ice-cream while pointing his big black toy gun at his fair-haired pal's temple. A small caption in the bottom right corner gave the necessary info for the exhibit. That's it. The shot and its title and its message were controversial enough but what happened was that a week after the billboards first appeared two boys in the city accidentally killed their siblings by trying to enact my photograph using their parents' real firearms. At the news I was appalled shocked shattered petrified paralyzed devastated traumatized. But: not only did I demand all twenty-five billboards be taken down immediately and disposed of not only did I destroy the negatives not only did I make a formal public apologetic declaration of artistic and ideological disownment of that disgraceful monstrosity I also made arrangements with my lawyer to provide the families with monetary and psychological support and heartfelt apologies in writing. And when some time later some kind of pundit on the tube declared that in his view the true culprits of those tragedies were the trigger-happy Second Amendment-loving parents who had left their firearms unattended or anyway within reach of their children I wrote to the TV station saying that although opposed to the dangerously high circulation of weapons in the US I took full responsibility for what had happened because however unwillingly I had inspired those children with my photograph because without my photograph displayed all over the city those children would have never taken their siblings' lives and ruined their own and those of their parents. And I did all this with a heavy heart because I believe in the power of art but I also believe in and feel charged with the great responsibility that power calls for. Unlike J. D. Salinger who after John Lennon's death could have or should have withdrawn his book from commerce just like he did with his early stories which he felt embarrassed about and therefore denied reprints and republications. But The Catcher in the Rye keeps selling pretty well to this day so why withdraw it right?

Now I do not know if my disorder my DID as they call it my Dissociative Identity Disorder for those who do not know what DID means and what used to be called Dual and then Multiple Personality Disorder is connected with my being a professional photographer but I have seriously thought about it and have reached the conclusion that perhaps since photography is an art that in a way disguises and separates essence from appearance the ego from the self or selves and since black-and-white photography which is the only art I create though I have taken some color shots for my own amusement since black-and-white photography has a slightly more as the name suggests dichotomous approach and therefore influence on how the photographer herself sees things life nature people the world I might have developed some sort of subconscious need to devise a doppelgänger to split myself into two or more. For example self-portraits like the ones of my 2008 solo show My cR.O.S.s to Bear show my own face and the smallest pores and spots and the unruly spiky hair growing unseen under the chin or along the jaw and show the idea the image I wanted to give and not necessarily my identity or personality be that single double or even multiple especially because in taking a self-portrait you are forced to split at least twofold in awareness: the artist concerned with light shadow composition focus angle and the subject who has to willy-nilly elect a pose whose choice derives from both deep and shallow considerations about oneself considerations which swing between self-imposed authenticity and authentic imposture a pose choice that forms as an answer to the simply unanswerable introspective question: What or whom with this pose this posture this stance this reproducible immobility this infinite reproducibility do I want to look like among my several selves? I do not know for certain and Dr. McVain has not been able to answer this question. In fact he keeps saying he does not believe what I tell him about my childhood and my parents especially my father and he says I must have repressed those ugly memories maybe because I was too scared to come to terms with them and I must have had Dr. McVain says a completely different childhood than the one I remember and recount a childhood full of incidents of probably abuse surely despair just like ninety percent of the people suffering from DID to which I remember replying that only because numbers stats percentage math simplified a situation it did not mean the situation was simple and that for sure I am not simple and I do not even content myself with belonging to the remaining ten percent for I am the wild variable of a bigger equation and my existence is a unique and complex algorithm an algorithm that resolved into its components does not generate a litany of distinct qualities flaws defects merits but creates a transcendental non-binary ontology whose uncharted alienness is the product of the unjust unjustified useless division of what was meant to remain united even in its doubleness and shadowy intricacy. *Shit Ros none of it makes sense but you sounded so sexy saying it. My god if we weren't driving I'd touch myself just replaying what you said in my head until ecstasy and orgasm seized us in one single sweaty embrace…* You are not that bad yourself. But wait I lost the thread…

Shit what the fuck is that?! Is that the police?

Damn it! Do they want us to pull over? Think so. So
shall we pull over or attempt an escape and ensue a
car chase in cinematic style? Marta? Marta?! Where
the fuck are you now that I need you?! Marta?! Hey!
Shit shit shit! I pull over and follow the officer as he
comes out of the car in his uniform and walks toward
me and steals a glance at my car's plates and when I
say my car I mean Joyce Finnegan's father's car this
station wagon with this chocking perfume of pepper
mint or whatever mint this is and who knows maybe
it is not even mint and the cop swaggers along the
line looking at my side mirror trying to catch my eye
or any jerky move and don't ask me why I start
picturing to fuck him and I don't even like people in
uniform still I see him as the personification of all
that I am not and this contrast this polarity this
antithesis kind of turns me on. He is broad-
shouldered and square-jawed and I like to assume
thick-skulled short-sighted and short-dicked but a
casual extempore and much-needed fuck
nonetheless… So he approaches and asks me to roll
down the window ma'am which I do and asks me to
produce my driver's license ma'am which I don't
because I don't have it anymore of course since the
day I walked into that nuthouse so I tell him I must
have forgotten it at home to which unsurprisingly he
replies with the usual formulaic not at all droll drill
about stepping outside the vehicle ma'am and
keeping my hands where he can see them and I

refrain from asking him if he would be able to see them had I slid them down his underpants and then I hear him speak over the radio saying Yes sir I found her. No sir just around the corner. Yes sir she's fine or at least she looks fine to me. Yes sir we'll be back there in no time. Back at the fucking loony bin! I want to shout but don't perhaps accustomed as I am at having Marta do the nasty dirty filthy talking and now Marta is nowhere to be found and when the cop asks me to get in the car which has all the while been beaming off flashing its red and blue lights giving the scene a head-turning urban touch and giving me an unusual and unasked-for spotlight so as I sit in the back of a police car a black and white as they call them which pleases me with wry glee for I have often been labeled as a black-and-white fundamentalist and now finally arrested for it! so as I sit in the back of a black and white for the first time in my life and we make a U-turn and drive back to the nuthouse or the funny farm as I heard Joyce call it once Joyce whose old father must have given the alarm and who can blame him? I note that Marta has disappeared exactly when I saw the red and blue lights which means she probably chickened out she withdrew she vanished and I do not know if that's a good or a bad thing… And then when we get through the gates and everything starts to look familiar habitual even comforting the hedge running along the perimeter the gravel crackling under the tires the trees the small

fenced off smoking area where patients who don't
smoke loiter as an act of pointless defiance when the
setting of my everyday life starts to replace the
mysterious thrilling unknown of my botched escape
though to be honest I had no idea where to go when
the setting starts to regain its pre-eminence I notice
Dr. McVain standing by the entrance with his hands
in his unbuttoned white coat pockets and I feel pretty
much the same way I felt when I got back home
from Southern Italy something like twenty years ago
and at the arrivals at JFK saw my father's face and
now on Dr. McVain's face who is not my father
though one could argue he is some kind of a father
figure to me hence my libidinal desire for him on his
face I see the hardly masked reproach the hardly
masked relief the hardly masked terror still deforming
his expression tensing his muscles tightening his
nerves revealing tension anxiety fear the long-lasting
effects of prolonged exposure to the masochistic and
typically parental practice of envisioning tragic
disastrous catastrophic scenarios. He moves forward
and as soon as I come out he hugs me and holds me
tight like my father did back then and with tears in
my eyes tears I did not know were waiting to trickle
down my cheeks I stutter and spittle Th-that's very
unp-professional of you doc and he chuckles a
relieved chuckle and says Thank god you're okay
Ros. Was afraid you had done something foolish.

Like posting hate-filled tweets with the hashtag

StopPredatorDrMcVain?

No something seriously foolish he says alluding to
suicide which is what Dr. McVain says I attempted on the
day I killed J. D. Salinger and that instead of the murder I
claim to have committed with Marta's help what I did that
day was to try to kill myself the ultimate trigger for my
pathologic disassociation the fictional event the fabricated
action the figmental genesis of my life *after* and through
which Dr. McVain believes I subconsciously managed to
split myself my ego my identity in two.

Don't worry doc I say. Like my father used to say
Dying is the last thing I wanna do in life.

Dr. McVain laughs and as we disengage I let the gym
bag thump to the ground and hear glass breaking. It
must be the framed photograph of my parents the color
portrait I took in their snowy backyard a month before
ending up here the decade-old photograph that shows
the way they used to look at me before my insanity broke
out before this whole big mess I live in the photograph
of our before when their eyes were moist with pride love
and encouragement and belief in their only daughter.
That photograph also shows the way they looked when
they used to visit me here with regularity the relaxed
faces of ageing parents finally at peace with their choices
until with time the intervals between one visit and the
next grew longer their faces gloomier our silences louder
and the distance between us more and more
unbridgeable. So picturing that picture now fragmented
pixelated censored by the shattered glass I see the way

they are withering away fading away blurring into one sweet loving memory. Like cosmic karmic galaxies in the ever-expanding universe my parents and I are receding from each other as the rest of humanity is and now our encounters our brief laconic exchanges our grim vignettes of soporific awkwardness are reiterated valedictory frames arranged like barbed wire by the intimist interpersonal intervalometer of my folly to create a deathly time-lapse photography of our decaying bodies of our bruised traumatized disenchanted detached crumbling lives…

Acknowledgements

My deepest thanks to my wife Pivia (without whom I would be nothing and nothing would be done) for her literary intuition her patience and her understanding. And to my daughters Aida and Frida for their support and visits which are the best breaks from work I could ever dream of. Huge thanks to Sam Ruddock at Story Machine for his sensibility and editorial help and for having picked this story as a winner. Thanks to my family and to Paul S. Brown and Steve Hendrix and Paolo Pedretti for their encouragement over the years. This book is also for you Olmo (??-??-2021).

The Stanley Kubrick quote on page 8 is from Penelope Houston and Philip Strick. "Modern Times: An Interview With Stanley Kubrick." *Sight and Sound* (Spring 1972): 62-66 in *The Stanley Kubrick Archives* edited by Alison Castle. Taschen Gmbh 2019 p. 532.

Thank you for supporting planet-friendly publishing

Story Machine seeks to have a net positive social and environmental impact. That means the environment and people's lives are actually better off for every book we print. Story Machine offsets our entire carbon footprint plus 10% through a www.ClimateCare.org programme. We are now investing in converting to use only 100% renewable energies and seeking out the most planet-positive means of shipping books to our readers.

The printing insustry is a huge polluter, requiring the use of huge amounts of water, toxic chemicals, and energy. Even FSC certified mix paper sources drive deforestation. That's why we are proud to be working with www.Seacort.net, a global leader in planet positive printing. Not only have they developed a waterless and chemical-free process, they use only 100% renewable energies, FSC certified recycled paper, and direct absolutely no waste to landfill. That's why they were crowned Europe's most sustainable SME in 2017, and have been recognised as one of the top three environmental printers in the world.

Planet-positive printing costs us a little more. But we think this is a small price to pay for a better world, today and in the future. If you agree, please share our message, and encourage other publishers and authors to commit to planet-positive printing. Stories can change the world. They deserve publishers that want to make sure they do. Together, we can make publishing more sustainable.